For RP, who encourages me to soar!—R.S.

MARGARET K. McELDERRY BOOKS • An imprint of Simon & Schuster Children's Publishing Division • 1230 Avenue of the Americas, New York, New York 10020 • Text copyright © 2019 by Rob Sanders • Illustrations copyright © 2019 by Helen Yoon • All rights reserved, including the right of reproduction in whole or in part in any form. • MARGARET K. McELDERRY BOOKS is a trademark of Simon & Schuster, Inc. • For information about special discounts for bulk purchases, please contact Simon & Schuster Special Sales at 1-866-506-1949 or business@simonandschuster.com. • The Simon & Schuster Speakers Bureau can bring authors to your live event. For more information or to book an event, contact the Simon & Schuster Speakers Bureau at 1-866-248-3049 or visit our website at www.simonspeakers.com. • Book design by Lauren Rille • The text for this book was set in Prater Sans. • The illustrations for this book were rendered in mixed media, and then compiled digitally. • Manufactured in China • 0619 SCP • First Edition • 10 9 8 7 6 5 4 3 2 1 • Library of Congress Cataloging-in-Publication Data • Names: Sanders, Rob, 1958– author. | Yoon, Helen, illustrator. • Title: Ball and Balloon / Rob Sanders ; illustrated by Helen Yoon. • Description: First edition. | New York : Margaret K. McElderry Books, [2019] | Summary: Ball wishes he could fly like Balloon, but when a boy arrives and sends Ball rolling, bouncing, and even soaring into the air, Balloon feels deflated. • Identifiers: LCCN 2018003251 (print) | ISBN 9781534425620 (hardcover) | ISBN 9781534425637 (eBook) • Subjects: | CYAC: Balls—Fiction. | Balloons—Fiction. | Envy—Fiction. | Play—Fiction. • Classification: LCC PZ7.S19785 Bal 2019 (print) | DDC [E]—dc23 • LC record available at https://lccn.loc.gov/2018003251

Written by Rob Sanders • Illustrated by Helen Yoon

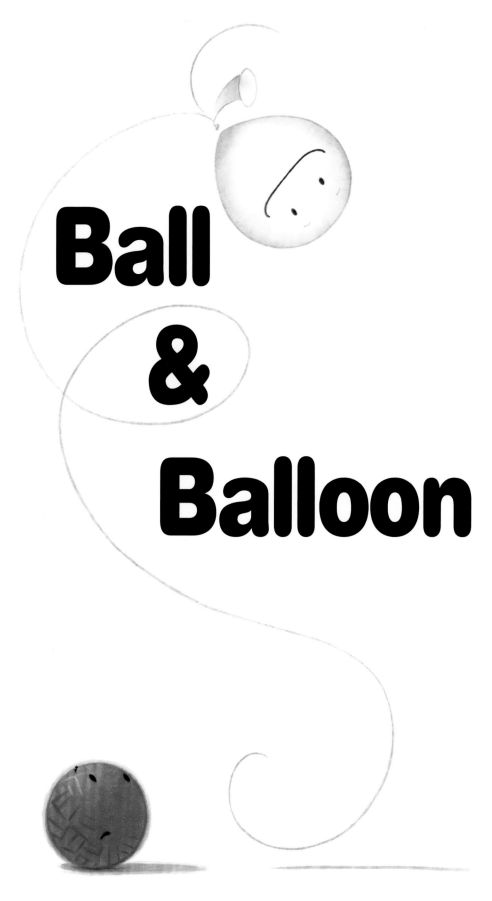

Ball
&
Balloon

Margaret K. McElderry Books • New York London Toronto Sydney New Delhi

G
ravity had Ball down.

Balloon laughed in the face of gravity.

Balloon swooped and swirled.
Ball sat and stared.
"How did you learn to fly?" Ball asked.

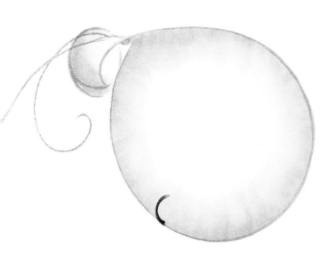

Balloon hadn't learned to fly.
It was just something inside him.

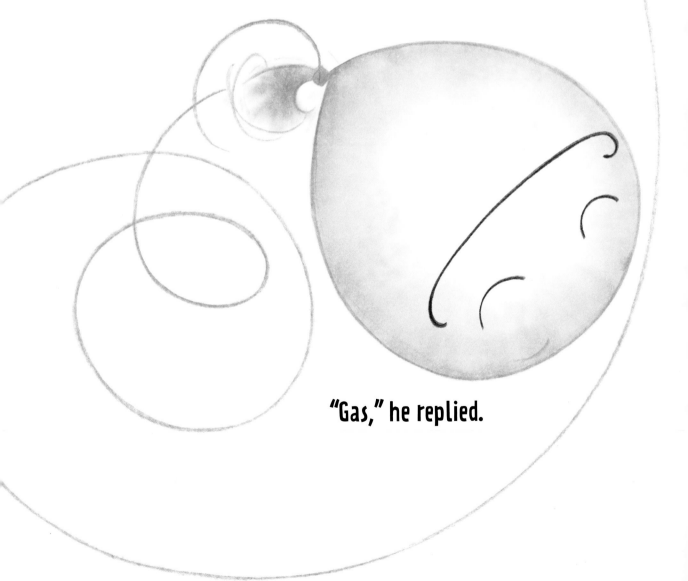

"Gas," he replied.

Ball wished he had gas.
He wished he were a balloon.
He wished he could fly.

He grunted.

He groaned.

And he tried to thrust himself into the air. . . .

Still grounded.

"Maybe I can't fly," Ball said. "But I'm a good roller."
"Show me," said Balloon.

Ball grunted.
He groaned.
He pushed off . . .

but he was
not on a roll.

And Balloon was
not impressed.

"I can bounce," said Ball.
"Oh, really?" Balloon said. "Prove it."

Ball grunted.

He groaned.

And he tried to bounce with all his might. . . .

Not a dribble.

Balloon looked down on Ball.
"The sky's the limit," he called. "Ta-ta, Ball!"
Balloon let loose and flew as high as he could.

Ball sat.

And sat some more.
And some more.
And some more.

Until finally . . .

someone arrived.

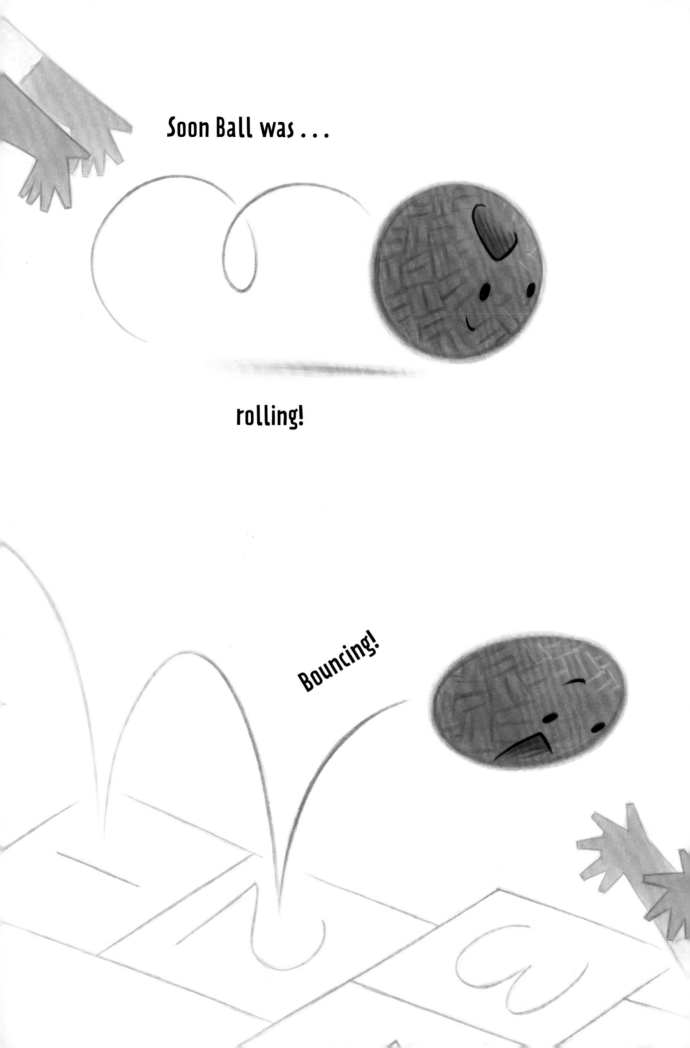

Soon Ball was . . .

rolling!

Bouncing!

And even flying through the air!

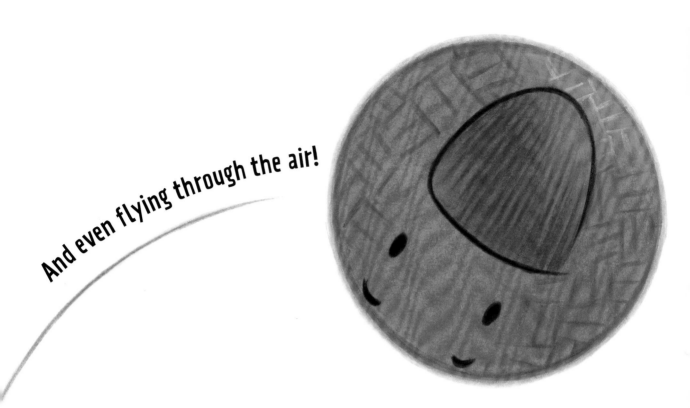

Balloon couldn't believe his eyes.

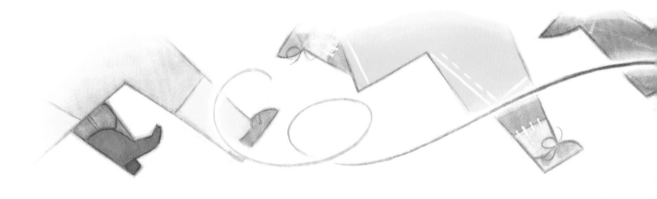

Ball swirled between feet,

sailed between hands,

SWOOSH

and swooshed to score.

"I'm so lucky," Ball said.
"So lucky to be a ball."

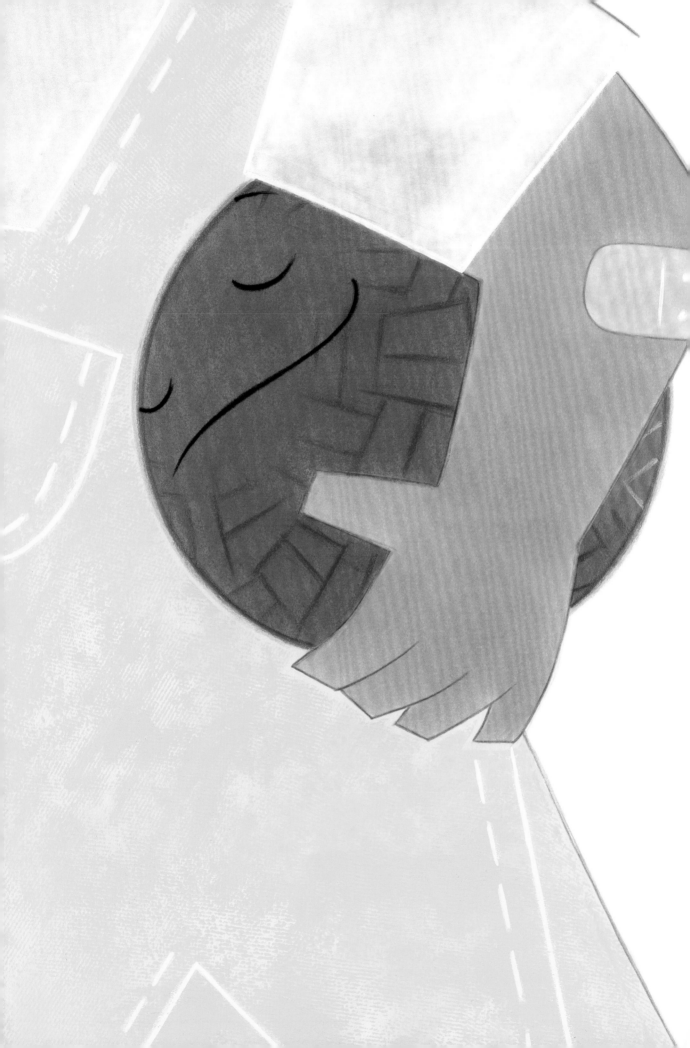

Someone held Ball close.
Ball felt something inside.
Maybe it was gas.
Maybe it was something else.

Then he heard a quiet voice.

"I wish I were a ball."
It was Balloon.
He was feeling a bit deflated.

Being a balloon might not
be that great after all.

Flying had its ups and downs.
Ball realized there were
worse things than gravity.

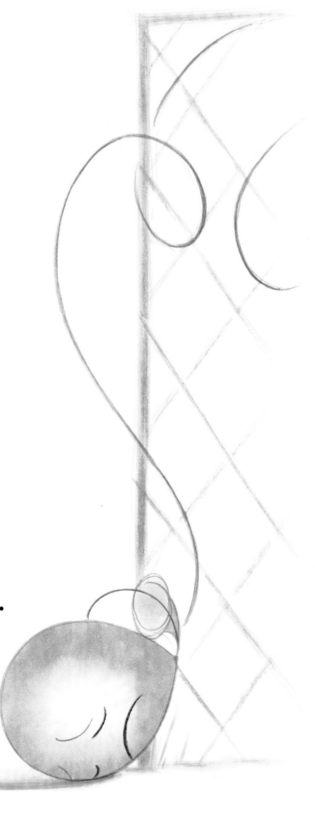

Ball grunted.

He groaned.

And . . .

he popped out from under
someone's arm
and bounced,
then rolled . . .

to Balloon.

Someone understood.